Adventures of Nino & Tenna
FOREST EXPLORER

Story by Ethan & Jonah Herald
Written by Brian Herald
Illustrated by Karine Makartichan

About this story: Ethan loves telling stories. He has been telling stories about this character Nino, and Nino's little sister Tenna, since he was about two years old. This is one of the stories he described.

A special note to readers: You may notice that Nino, Tenna, and Puppy Dog look a little different in this story than others in the series. That's because Ethan and Jonah like to see different designs in their stories. These characters were created in their imagination, so they look however Ethan and Jonah say they look at the time!

Third Edition

It was a bright, warm morning, and Nino could think of nothing better to do than to take a walk in the woods near his house.

He started his walk at a trail right off the sidewalk. He did not see the sign that said "Not An Entrance" because the small sign was covered by tree branches.

Once he started down the trail, Nino ventured off of it once in a while to look closely at giant old trees, and colorful flowers.

Sometimes, when he moved a big rock, he saw worms and other insects scuttling along.
They might have been surprised by the bright sunlight, he thought.
Nino wondered how dark it was under a rock. He was a little too big to fit under a rock, so he closed
his eyes and then opened them as fast as he could, trying to surprise himself with the bright sunlight.
Maybe this is what it is liked for an insect when a rock is picked up.

Nino had been walking for only a few minutes before he felt like he was far into the woods. There were some scents in the air that he recognized. He could smell the trees, and smell the dirt, and sometimes, he could even smell the scent of smoke. That smell reminded him of winter nights at his home when his family would have a fire.

After a while, Nino noticed that the sunlight in the sky was not as bright as it had been before.
He decided it was time to head back home.
He turned around on the trail and started walking back towards the entrance.
As he looked down the trail, Nino could see that it led back to the entrance where he started,
but now there was a gate blocking the way.

8

Nino ran up to the gate and found it locked shut. He tried shaking the gate and calling for help.
He saw that the sky was getting darker and darker,
and it was getting harder for him to see through the trees around him.

Nino took a couple of steps back away from the gate to think about what he should do next. He took a deep breath and realized that he could still smell the scent of smoke in the air.

As the sky got darker and darker, Nino saw a bright spot in the distance.
A spot in the sky that was almost glowing.
He walked towards it to find out what it could be.

Nino walked closer to the bright spot, and he realized that it wasn't in the sky at all. It was in the trees! And that scent of smoke was not just his imagination-it was smoke from a real fire!

Nino yelled for help, but he wasn't sure if anyone could hear him besides the trees, and the flowers, and the insects. He yelled and he yelled. He even grabbed handfuls of dirt and tried to throw it onto the flames to smother them, but he needed more help. Then, Nino heard what sounded like a siren. And it got louder, and louder, and louder.

Suddenly, out of the darkness, fire truck after fire truck raced down the trail towards the fire. Nino felt relieved that help had arrived.

When the fire trucks stopped to put out the fire, one of the firefighters saw Nino. The firefighter wrapped up Nino in a blanket and carried him to a fire truck. He cheered on the firefighters as they drenched the flames with water.

After the fire was out, the firefighters drove Nino back to his house.
He was so glad that the fire was out, and he was so excited to be riding in a real rescue fire truck.

When they returned Nino to his home, the firefighters thanked him for being so observant and for doing his very best to help protect the forest.
They told Nino's sister, Tenna, that Nino had acted like a hero.

When the Fire Chief asked Nino about how the forest fire had started, he explained to the firefighters that a dragon flew down from the sky and blew flames out of its mouth, and that's what started the fire.

The firefighters chuckled at Nino's exciting story and said that fires can start a lot of different ways.

Back inside his house, after the firefighters had left, Nino told Tenna and Puppy Dog
all about his day exploring the trees, and the flowers, and the insects.
And he told them about how he recognized the scent of smoke in the air,
and how he spotted the flames from far away.
Tenna and Puppy Dog were very proud of Nino, and Nino was so happy to be home safe with them.

THE END

THANKS FOR READING OUR STORIES!

My name's Brian. I am capturing the stories my sons tell me and am happy to share them with you. These stories aim to entertain, educate, and remind us of the fun things we did as children through curiosity, creativity, and exploration.

My son Ethan started telling me stories about this character Nino, and Nino's sister Tenna, when he was about two years old. I started jotting them down and the Adventures of Nino and Tenna series was born! Now Ethan's brother Jonah is part of the story creation team. Together, the two come up with the ideas for all of the stories in this series.

As for my writing experience, I've been writing professionally over than 15 years, mostly instructional and educational materials, and am now proud to bring to the world this fun adventure series.

WHAT WILL YOU READ NEXT?

Our stories are available in paperback, e-book, and audiobook!

THERE'S MORE WAITING FOR YOU!

Nino & Tenna Reader Team members receive a downloadable and printable **Activity Book** based on this story, including lots and LOTS of coloring pages, maze activities, and more!

As a **Reader Teamer**, you'll also receive our monthly Kid's Calendar, which is jam-packed with special occasions for kids to enjoy.

Scan this QR Code to get access to now!

SO WHAT'D YA THINK?

If you and your child enjoyed this story, could you please let someone else know about it? Maybe tell a friend or leave a review somewhere? We'd really appreciate that!

Adventures of Nino & Tenna
FOREST EXPLORER

FIRE SAFETY TOPICS

Forest Explorer is a made-up story, and is not an example of what to do if you happen upon a fire in real life. Discuss these topics with your kids to help keep their adventures safe!

PLAN AHEAD
Have a plan before you even see a fire. Know where to go for help.

STAY AWAY
Stay a safe distance away from flames.

GET HELP
Always seek help, and let firefighters put out the fire.

TALK ABOUT IT
Discuss fire safety regularly.

TAKE A FIELD TRIP
Visit your local fire station. Meet the firefighters, explore the equipment, and learn about fire safety.

Made in United States
North Haven, CT
20 November 2022

27016298R00018